# The CAROUSEL

## LIZ ROSENBERG · JIM LaMARCHE

VOYAGER BOOKS    HARCOURT BRACE & COMPANY    *San Diego  New York  London*

Requests for permission to make copies of any part of the work should be mailed to:
Permissions Department, Harcourt Brace & Company, 6277 Sea Harbor Drive,
Orlando, Florida 32887-6777.

First Voyager Books edition 1998
*Voyager Books* is a registered trademark of Harcourt Brace & Company.

The Library of Congress has cataloged the hardcover edition as follows:
Rosenberg, Liz. The carousel/written by Liz Rosenberg; illustrated by Jim
LaMarche.—1st ed. p. cm. Summary: Two sisters find that the horses of a broken
carousel have come alive in the rain. ISBN 0-15-200853-5 hc. ISBN 0-15-201887-5 pb.
[1. Merry-go-round—Fiction. 2. Sisters—Fiction. 3. Horses—Fiction.]
I. LaMarche, Jim, ill. II. Title.
PZ7.R71894Car 1995b [E]—dc20 94-47323

F E D C B A

Printed in Singapore

The illustrations in this book were done in acrylic washes
with colored pencil on Arches watercolor paper.
The calligraphy was done by Georgia Deaver.
The text type was set in Stempel Garamond by Thompson Type,
San Diego, California.
Color separations by Bright Arts, Ltd., Singapore
Printed and bound by Tien Wah Press, Singapore
This book was printed on Arctic matte art paper.
Production supervision by Stanley Redfern and Jane Van Gelder
Designed by Camilla Filancia and Patrick Collins

*To my sister Ellen, who showed me the path*
*—L. R.*

*To Carl and Peggyann, Mary and George, thank you for always being there*
*—J. L.M.*

The time my sister and I saw the horses it was gray-skied, twilight — but warm because there had been a February thaw that day.

She picked me up after her band practice, and I teased her to stop at the park, even though we had things to do: homework and getting supper ready for my father.

So we turned right instead of left, and walked into the park through a ring of old oak trees.

It began to drizzle, raining lightly on the swings and the slides, and I thought my sister would head for home. Instead she took my hand in one hand, and swung her flute case in the other.

"The horses are asleep," she said in a whisper.

I smiled, because that was something our mother used to say: that the carousel horses slept all winter and woke in spring. But ours had been broken a long time.

We heard the raindrops striking the metal slides. The canvas over the carousel pavilion flapped in the wind — and then we heard a strange sound. A long whinnying noise.

We hurried closer to the carousel, and pulled the heavy white canvas aside.

Inside, the carousel horses were moving around, clopping their hooves, as alive as my sister or me. Their harnesses chimed like Christmas bells.

I recognized my favorite horse right away, the silvery gray mare. Whenever I rode the carousel, I raced for that mare. I knew everything about her by heart — her red and yellow jewelled saddle and gold tassels.

I jumped on her back the way I had a hundred times before.

"Wait!" my sister called to me, but we were off. My sister climbed on a black-and-white striped zebra and rode after us.

The mare broke into a run as soon as she reached the air.

We circled the band shell
and raced between the swings.
Higher and higher we flew.
Faster, and a little more reckless.
"Don't you dare go near that
swimming pool!" my sister yelled.

The others galloped close
behind. They threw back their
heads and snorted white clouds
of breath.

The big white Lippizaners
leapt back and forth over the
empty swimming pool, their
backs gleaming like snowy
mountains.

All of the horses ran harder and wilder.

One stallion kicked over a park bench, knocking it backward to the ground. Another sent a trash can spinning dizzily through the air.

"They're wild because they are broken," my sister said, and we both watched for a minute.

" — Maybe Mom's tool kit?" I asked.

Our mother had been someone who could fix anything, from leaky faucets to broken porch lights and bannisters. Sometimes she'd take apart the washing machine or toaster, just for fun, and put it back together while I played on the floor next to her.

Mom's red toolbox was still kept out in the garage, along with her bicycle and some of her old clothes.

"I'll go," I said quickly.

"We'll *all* go," my sister said.

It was raining harder. The horses ran separately now, cantering down the side streets to our house, a few blocks away.

I sprinted to the back of the garage and found the toolbox. It was covered with dust, but the tools inside were still shining. "Take good care of your tools," my mother had said, "and they'll take good care of you."

Lightning flashed close by. A few of the horses reared up, panicky, ready to bolt.

"Hurry," my sister said. "Hurry!"

We raced back to the park, plunging through puddles. Thunder rumbled all around us.

Inside the pavilion, I worked till I had the carousel machinery laid out in pieces, like the inside of a clock. My hands were clumsy because I hadn't handled any of those tools in a long time: the wrench, the screwdriver, needle-nosed pliers.

I held a flashlight the size of a pen and shone it carefully on every piece.

At last I found something small and silver. A bolt that had fallen into the machinery. I worked it loose and held it up in the air.

"It will work now."

But the horses had gone mad. They ran wild from one swing set to the other, crashed into the wire fence. Two spotted ponies began to fight over a paper bag filled with leftover lunch food, slashing at each other through the air.

My sister sat tall and straight on the zebra, holding her flute case. She was watching the horses the same way she sometimes watched me.

Then she took out her flute from the flute case, fitted the pieces together, and began to play.

The horses slowed a little, ran in a wide circle.

She played "Claire de Lune"— the song my mother used to play when we couldn't sleep at night.

The horses moved slower and slower, almost in a dance, lifting their hooves high.

One by one they jumped up onto their places on the carousel. Each knew exactly where to stand.

I buried my face in the mare's silvery neck. She smelled like new-mown grass and my mother's old wool coat.

"Come on," my sister said, not impatiently. She hated tearful scenes.

My father's car was pulling into the driveway just as we reached the house. He got out looking tired and worried, pushing the wet hair back from his forehead. "What were you girls doing out so late?" he asked.

My sister and I exchanged glances. We were soaked and shivering.

"We walked to the park," she told him.

His face brightened then, a little.

"Your mother used to say that park was magical in the rain." He even smiled.

He put up his big black umbrella and we stood there for a minute, all three of us, safe inside the umbrella, under the shining porch light. And then we went inside.